BEEN THERE AND BACK